HAVING A PICNIC

With love to Roger

HAVING A PICNIC
Sarah Garland

PUFFIN BOOKS

Off for a picnic.

Into the park.

Up the hill. . .

to look at the view.

Down to the pond. . .

to feed the ducks.

Where's the picnic?

Here it is!

Who's this?

Look out!

They've taken the buns!

Have a good picnic!